THE BEST·THING ABOUT VALENTINES

♥ By ELEANOR HUDSON
ILLUSTRATED By MARY C. MELCHER

SCHOLASTIC INC.

Cartwheel BOOKS®

New York Toronto London Auckland Sydney
Mexico City New Delhi Hong Kong Buenos Aires

To Abigail, Addy, Chloe, Christina, Elizabeth, Jennifer, Jessica, Jillian, Laura, Melissa, Molly, Nina, and Rebecca
—E.H.

To All My Dear Family and Friends and Most Favorite Valentine, David
—M.C.M.

ISBN 0-439-52109-2

Text copyright © 2004 by Scholastic Inc.
Illustrations copyright © 2004 by Mary C. Melcher.
All rights reserved. Published by Scholastic Inc.
SCHOLASTIC, CARTWHEEL BOOKS, and associated logos
are trademarks and/or registered trademarks of Scholastic Inc.

Library of Congress Cataloging-in-Publication Data
Hudson, Eleanor.
The best thing about valentines / by Eleanor Hudson ; illustrated by Mary C. Melcher.
p. cm.
"Cartwheel Books."
Summary: A child describes the fun of making, giving, and receiving valentines.
ISBN 0-439-52109-2 (pbk.)
[1. Valentines—Fiction. 2. Valentine's Day—Fiction. 3. Stories in rhyme.] I. Melcher, Mary, ill. II. Title.
PZ8.3.H8565Be 2004
[E]—dc21   2003007836

10 9 8 7 6 5 4 3 2   04 05 06 07 08
Printed in the U.S.A. 23 • First printing, January 2004

Valentines, valentines,
big ones and small—

I love making valentines.
I love it all!
Cutting paper and lace,

smearing glue sticks
and paste.

I use every scrap.
There's nothing
I waste!

Tying pink ribbons,

scattering glitter.

I always clean up

and try not to litter.

Valentines,
valentines,
big ones and small—
I love sending valentines.
I love it all!

I drop some
in the mailbox
right on my street.

Some others are mailed

with a yummy sweet treat.

Some valentines are
delivered by hand.

Others take longer
to cross our big land.

I bring more
valentines to school
for my friends.

We put them in boxes and,
when the class ends,

our teacher hands valentines
out one by one.

Then we give her a HUGE
valentine—so much fun!

Though it's great
to make valentines
and give them away...

I love *getting* valentines
on Valentine's Day!

Dear Parent:

Congratulations! Your child is taking the first steps on an exciting journey. The destination? Independent reading!

STEP INTO READING® will help your child get there. The program offers five steps to reading success. Each step includes fun stories and colorful art. There are also Step into Reading Sticker Books, Step into Reading Math Readers, Step into Reading Write-In Readers, Step into Reading Phonics Readers, and Step into Reading Phonics First Steps! Boxed Sets—a complete literacy program with something for every child.

Learning to Read, Step by Step!

Ready to Read   Preschool–Kindergarten
• big type and easy words • rhyme and rhythm • picture clues
For children who know the alphabet and are eager to begin reading.

Reading with Help   Preschool–Grade 1
• basic vocabulary • short sentences • simple stories
For children who recognize familiar words and sound out new words with help.

Reading on Your Own   Grades 1–3
• engaging characters • easy-to-follow plots • popular topics
For children who are ready to read on their own.

Reading Paragraphs   Grades 2–3
• challenging vocabulary • short paragraphs • exciting stories
For newly independent readers who read simple sentences with confidence.

Ready for Chapters   Grades 2–4
• chapters • longer paragraphs • full-color art
For children who want to take the plunge into chapter books but still like colorful pictures.

STEP INTO READING® is designed to give every child a successful reading experience. The grade levels are only guides. Children can progress through the steps at their own speed, developing confidence in their reading, no matter what their grade.

Remember, a lifetime love of reading starts with a single step!

Thomas the Tank Engine & Friends

A BRITT ALLCROFT COMPANY PRODUCTION

Based on The Railway Series by The Reverend W Awdry

© 2004 Gullane (Thomas) LLC

Thomas the Tank Engine & Friends and Thomas & Friends are trademarks of
Gullane Entertainment Inc.
Thomas the Tank Engine & Friends is Reg. U.S. Pat. TM Off.

A HIT Entertainment Company

All rights reserved under International and Pan-American Copyright Conventions. Published in
the United States by Random House Children's Books, a division of Random House, Inc., and
simultaneously in Canada by Random House of Canada Limited, Toronto.

www.stepintoreading.com
www.thomasthetankengine.com

Educators and librarians, for a variety of teaching tools, visit us at
www.randomhouse.com/teachers

Library of Congress Cataloging-in-Publication Data
James goes buzz, buzz / illustrated by Richard Courtney. — 1st ed.
p. cm. — (Step into reading; Step 2)
"Based on The railway series by the Rev. W. Awdry"
SUMMARY: James, a red train engine, tries to get rid of a group of bees that are plaguing him.
ISBN 0-375-82860-5 (trade) — ISBN 0-375-92860-X (lib. bdg.)
[1. Railroads—Trains—Fiction. 2. Bees—Fiction.] I. Courtney, Richard, 1955– ill. II. Awdry, W.
III. Series: Step into reading. Step 2 book.
PZ7.J1556 2004   [E]—dc22   2003020090

Printed in the United States of America
First Edition 10 9 8

STEP INTO READING, RANDOM HOUSE, and the Random House colophon are registered trademarks
of Random House, Inc.

STEP INTO READING®
STEP 2

James Goes Buzz, Buzz

Based on *The Railway Series*
by the Rev. W. Awdry

Illustrated by Richard Courtney

Random House 🏠 New York

It was a sunny day.
Chirp! Chirp!
sang the birds.
Buzz! Buzz!
hummed the bees.

Trevor the Tractor Engine
was hard at work.

Chug! Chug!
James pulled up.
"Hello, Trevor,"
said James.
"You look as busy
as a bee."

"I am!" said Trevor.

Buzz! Buzz!

"What is that noise?"

asked James.

8

"Bees," said Trevor.

"I am taking this beehive

to the station."

Buzz! Buzz!

buzzed the bees.

"Bees are very loud!"
said James.
"Do not make them mad,"
said Trevor.
"They may sting you!"

"Hmmmph!" said James. "I am not scared of a bunch of bees!" James puffed off.

The next day,
James chugged into
the station.
He saw boxes
and bundles
and bags.
And there was
the beehive!

People rushed
this way and that.
BUMP!
A porter bumped
into the beehive!

The beehive broke!

Buzz! Buzz!

The bees buzzed

around the station.

15

Buzz! Buzz!
The bees buzzed
around James.
"Buzz buzz off!"
said James.
The bees
did not listen.

The bees buzzed onto
James' hot boiler.
One of the bees
burned his foot.
Buzz! Buzz! Buzz!
The bee was angry.

He stung James
on the nose!

"Eeeeeeeeek,"
tooted James.
"Bad bee!"
James tried to make
the bees buzz off.

21

Chug! Chug!
James chugged
out of the station.

Whoosh!
He spun around
on the turntable.
Buzz! Buzz!
The bees liked the breeze.

Splash!
He tried to wash
them off.
Buzz! Buzz!
The bees took a bath.

Puff! Puff!
James blew smoke
at the bees.
Buzz! Buzz!
The bees did not budge.

27

James had an idea.

He turned around.

He chugged back
to find Trevor.

Buzz! Buzz!

The bees were home.

They buzzed back

into a beehive.

"Good bees!" said James.

"Goodbye, bees!"

If you can recognize familiar words and sound out new words with help, look for these Step into Reading books:

ALL STUCK UP
BARBIE: A DAY AT THE FAIR ✿
BARBIE: LOST AND FOUND ✿
BARBIE: ON THE ROAD ✿ ✎
BARBIE: TWO PRINCESSES ✿
BEARS ARE CURIOUS
BEEF STEW
THE BERENSTAIN BEARS BY THE
    SEA
THE BERENSTAIN BEARS
    CATCH THE BUS
BONES
BUZZ'S BACKPACK ADVENTURE ✪
CAT AT BAT
CAT ON ICE
CAT ON THE MAT   ·
COUNTING SHEEP ✧
DAVID AND THE GIANT
DINOSAUR BABIES
A DOLLAR FOR PENNY ✧
A DOZEN DOGS ✧
THE EARLY BIRD
FIVE SILLY FISHERMEN ✧
HAPPY BIRTHDAY, THOMAS! ➤
HOME, STINKY HOME ✪
HONEYBEES
I LOVE YOU, MAMA ✪
IS IT HANUKKAH YET?
JAMES GOES BUZZ, BUZZ ➤
LITTLE CRITTER SLEEPS OVER
LITTLE CRITTER'S
    THE BEST PRESENT
MICE ARE NICE
MOUSE MAKES MAGIC ♦
MY BEST FRIEND IS OUT OF THIS
    WORLD
MY LOOSE TOOTH
MY NEW BOY

MY NEW PET IS THE GREATEST
A NEW BRAIN FOR IGOR
NO MAIL FOR MITCHELL
NOAH'S ARK
ONE HUNDRED SHOES ✧
PEANUT
PIE RATS AHOY!
PINOCCHIO'S NOSE GROWS ✪
PIZZA PAT
P. J. FUNNYBUNNY CAMPS OUT
P. J. FUNNYBUNNY'S BAG OF TRICKS
PLATYPUS!
POLAR BABIES
A PONY FOR A PRINCESS ✪
POOH'S EASTER EGG HUNT ✪
POOH'S GRADUATION ✪
POOH'S HALLOWEEN PUMPKIN ✪
POOH'S HONEY TREE ✪
QUICK, QUACK, QUICK!
RAILROAD TOAD
READY? SET. RAYMOND!
RICHARD SCARRY'S
    THE WORST HELPER EVER
SILLY SARA ♦
SIR SMALL AND THE DRAGONFLY
THE STATUE OF LIBERTY
SURPRISE FOR A PRINCESS ✪
THE TAIL OF LITTLE SKUNK
THE TEENY TINY WOMAN
THOMAS AND THE SCHOOL TRIP ➤
TIGER IS A SCAREDY CAT
TOAD ON THE ROAD
TWO FINE LADIES HAVE A TIFF
TWO FINE LADIES: TEA FOR THREE
WANT A RIDE?
WHAT A MESS!
WHISKERS
WHOSE FEET?

✿   A Barbie Reader
✪   A Disney Reader
✧   A Math Reader
♦   A Phonics Reader
➤   A Thomas the Tank Engine Reader
✎   A Write-In Reader

STEP INTO READING

reading with help

It's time for YOU!
Pick your favorite
spot to read.
This is going to be
a great book!

What this book is about . . .
James Goes Buzz, Buzz
Bees are very small. James is a
splendid engine. He is too important to be
bothered by some bees! Or is he?

Learning to Read, Step by Step!

Ready to Read   **Preschool–Kindergarten**

Reading with Help   **Preschool–Grade 1**
Does your child recognize familiar words on sight and
sound out new words with help? Step 2 is just right.
Basic Vocabulary • Short Sentences • Simple Stories

Reading on Your Own   **Grades 1–3**

Reading Paragraphs   **Grades 2–3**

To learn about
all the Steps,
turn to page 1.

Chapters   **Grades 2–4**

Our Price $2.99

50299

ISBN 978-0-375-82860-7
9 780375 828607

thomasthetankengine.com

RANDOM HOUSE
www.stepintoreading.com

I, <u>Mrs. Sandfort</u>,
(Your Name)

have read this book

once,

twice,

again and again!